This Book belongs to

....

Good Friends Stick Together

Diane Tomczak

Illustrations by Blueberry Illustrations

For good friends everywhere ...

"Good friends will stick with you until you're unstuck." Winnie the Pooh/ A.A. Milne

Burs are covered with little hooks that stick to practically everything. If you've ever hiked through a field, chances are you've come home with bristly burs stuck to your pant leg or your dog's fur.

What does a bur feel like? Touch the straps on your sneakers. That material is Velcro, and it's what keeps your shoes fastened. Burs grab hold just like that strap which is why they're called nature's Velcro.

The wind was ripe
for branch bobbing.
Swooshing us up
Swirling us down

Swinging us left

Sweeping us right …

I reached for Spike,
but in a crow's cry,
a wag had whisked
him away.

I missed my bobbing buddy.
I watched and I waited
for the twice-a-day dog
to bring back Spike,
but my favorite bur
was not aboard.

"I WILL find you,"
I whispered on the wind.
There was only one way.

I shook off the dew
and leaned a little,
then a little more.

The twice-a-day dog
began as a bitty blur,
growing big-**BIGGER**.
His paws pounded the path
loud-**LOUDER**,

letting me know
it was time
to hook and hitch
my ride
in

3
2
1

"GOTCHA!"

We jumped
and chased.

"Spike, are you near?"

We swam
and raced.

"What about here?"

From cuff
to canvas

'Did you come this way, too?"

From canvas
to case.

"Am I closer to you?"

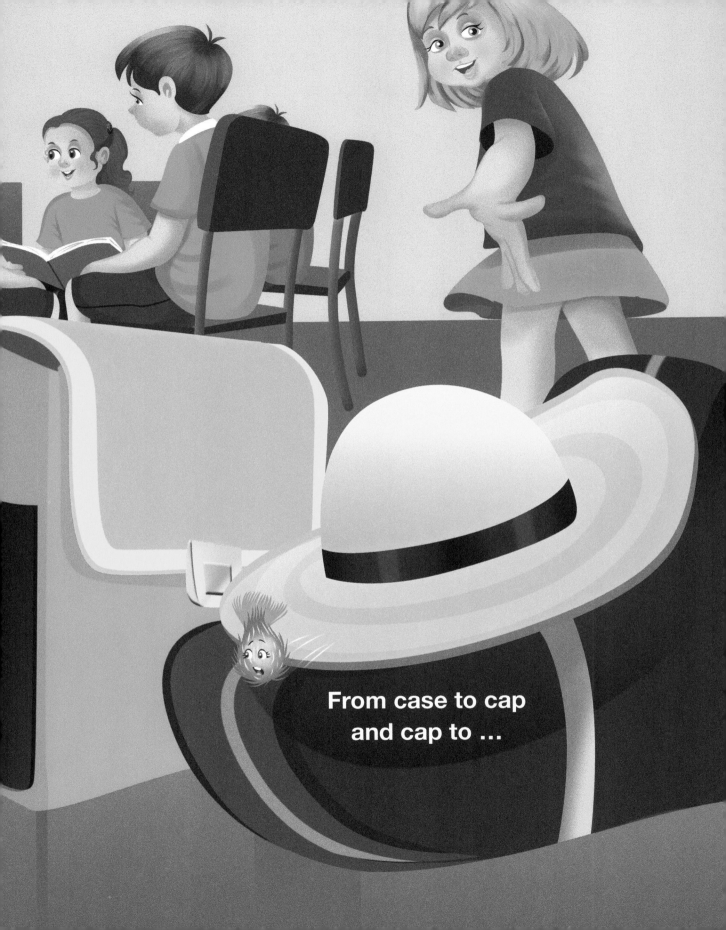

From case to cap
and cap to ...

... CAN!

"Now, what do I do?"

Apple cores and broken crayons,
rumpled scraps and pencil curls,
stale crusts and cookie crumbs,
and talking tissue

TALKING tissue?

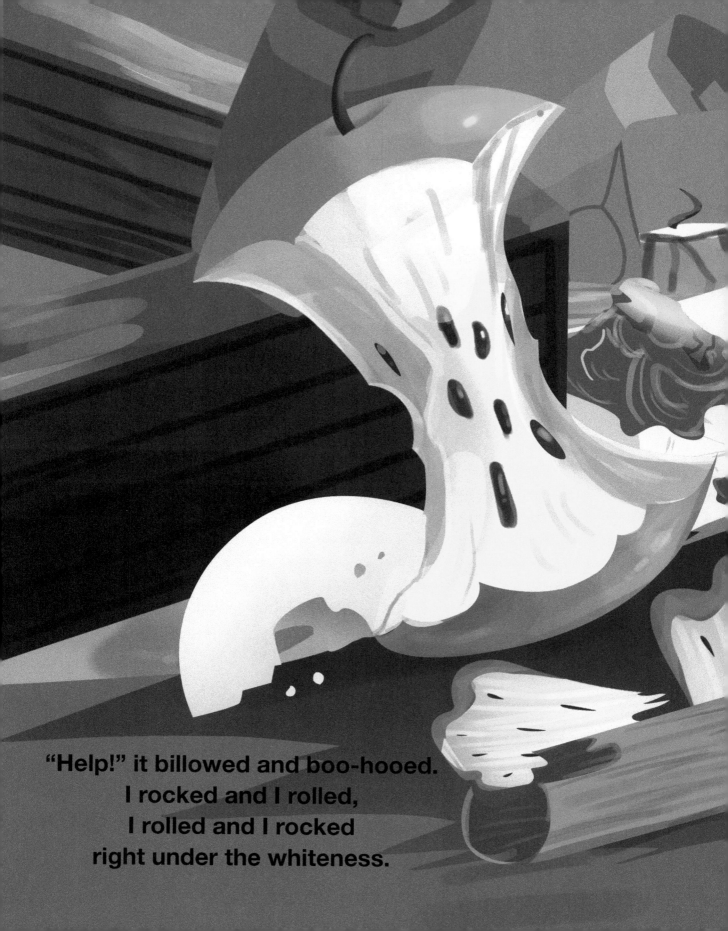

"Help!" it billowed and boo-hooed.
I rocked and I rolled,
I rolled and I rocked
right under the whiteness.

"Spike!"
"Tag!"
We hollered,
hugged,
and hoorayed

'til a tilt and a toss
tumbled us toward
a taxi for two.

"Look, Spike! Our ride!"
We leaned left and latched
before surely switching

from canvas
to cuff

to tick-tocking tail
until we were home.

Good friends stick together.

A former teacher, *Diane Tomczak* has written award-winning haiku and enjoys playing fingerstyle baritone ukulele. She spent much of her childhood hiking through the Michigan woods with her family, exploring trails and picking huckleberries. "Some days my dog and I would return home with bundles of little burs stuck to us. Although we tried to pick most of them off, I'm sure we missed a couple, just like Tag and Spike, who went on to have some wild adventures of their own." Diane and her husband live in Bay City, Michigan.

CPSIA information can be obtained
at www.ICGtesting.com
Printed in the USA
BVHW022259060222
628274BV00005B/181

9 780578 336619